Where has Daddy gone?

Trudy Osman
Pictures by Joanna Carey

Introduction by Dr David Pithers

MAMMOTH

First published in Great Britain 1990
by William Heinemann Ltd
Published 1994 by Mammoth
an imprint of Reed Consumer Books Ltd
Michelin House, 81 Fulham Road, London SW3 6RB
and Auckland, Melbourne, Singapore and Toronto

10 9 8 7 6 5

Text copyright © Trudy Osman 1990
Illustrations copyright © Joanna Carey 1990

ISBN 0 7497 1583 9

A CIP catalogue record for this title
is available from the British Library

Produced by Mandarin Offset Ltd
Printed and bound in China

Each year thousands of children have to deal with the separation of their parents or other close adults. Although it is impossible to include all the factors which may be involved in a particular family, some of the main themes are presented in this book by Trudy Osman, written from personal experience and professional concern.

The world in which children grow up is not stable, predictable or just; they cannot always be protected from painful or difficult experiences and indeed, to try to protect them from their own pain is to court emotional damage far more severe than allowing them to work through what is there.

However, many adults find it difficult to accept children's pain, and so the message we often inadvertently give them when they are hurt is that we don't want to know about it. Children can thus feel pressured into not expressing their feelings, either because they don't know how to, or because they believe that they will be ignored, rejected, misunderstood or even punished if they reveal what they are really experiencing. It is only because we sometimes fail to look beneath the surface that children seem to 'cope with loss far better than adults.'

Read with a responsible adult, a book like this can provide a well-informed focus for conversation with a child. It does not avoid difficult issues, but tackles them in a relaxed style and with super illustrations. I love that cat!

Although the break-up of an adult relationship can never be the responsibilty of a child, children take on guilt because they are kept in the dark and do not understand. I warmly commend this book because it can help to spare many children this unnecessary pain.

Dr David Pithers
Child Psychotherapist
National Children's Home
London

When I was little, Daddy used to hug me when he came home from work. Mum and Dad were very happy with each other.

On Saturdays, we used to go shopping together. Daddy sometimes bought Mum a book and something for me to play with. My favourite present was a football. Daddy's favourite present from Mum was a new camera. It was for his birthday.

Mum took lots of photographs as I got bigger, especially when we were happy and having fun.

When I was older, I sometimes heard Mum and Dad arguing at night, when I should have been asleep.

Mum and Dad would shout at each other when they were angry but, usually, they would be friends again by morning.

One morning, Mum said Dad had gone away.
It was a big shock for me.
Mum cried a lot. Then she explained that
Mummy and Daddy couldn't make each other
happy any more, so they had decided to live
in separate houses.
She said that they were both very sad
about it.

Later Daddy came to collect his clothes.
He hugged me, then he went away.
I felt very muddled up.
I wanted to cry but I couldn't. So I tried to be good and to cheer Mum up. Sometimes it was difficult.

The next Saturday, we didn't go shopping.
I waited for my Daddy but he didn't come.
I played with my football in the garden but it
burst on the railings. I cried and cried.
Mum hugged me.

I asked Mum, "Where has Daddy gone?" She explained that Mum and Dad would always live in different houses now, because they didn't love each other enough to live together.

Mum said it would be very sad and upsetting for everyone at first, but things would gradually get better.

I still have a Mum and a Dad who love me, but they just don't live in the same place now.

It was very strange, not seeing Daddy every day. I missed him a lot at first. Sometimes I felt angry with Mum and Dad because they didn't want to live together any more, but mostly I just felt very sad.

Mum said that the next time I saw Daddy I would have lots to tell him, and perhaps we could swap some photographs of the things we had done and the places we had visited.

Mum and I took care of each other.
Sometimes I helped to wash up, and I
tidied my room.
Mum bought some new wallpaper for my
bedroom and tried to put it on by herself.
I helped her but we got in a real mess with
the glue. Even the cat was all sticky!
It took a long time to finish the room, but we
had a lot of fun.

Mum made a special board for my
photographs.
She said it was a pity Dad wasn't there to
take a picture of the poor sticky cat!
Wallpapering wasn't as easy as when Daddy
did it, but in the end it looked really good.

When Dad was settled in his new house,
Mum said I could visit him.
At first it felt very strange, but I soon felt at
home because Daddy hadn't changed.
He gave me a big hug as soon as I got there.

That night, when Mum was tucking me in, I asked her if I could live at Daddy's house. Mum explained that Mum and Dad had talked about it, and they'd decided that it was better for me to live with Mum until I am more grown-up.

I thought it was probably a good idea – Daddy's cooking isn't as nice as Mum's!

Mum sometimes looks sad but she doesn't cry now.
Last night, Grandpa came to babysit so that Mum could go out with her friends.
She seemed happy again.
I like being with my Grandpa.